Christopher & Caroline in India

Joanne Grady Huskey

To order additional copies of this book, contact:
Xlibris
844-714-8691
www.Xlibris.com
Orders@Xlibris.com

ISBN: Softcover   979-8-3694-1281-7
        EBook   979-8-3694-1282-4

Print information available on the last page

Rev. date: 12/05/2023

DEDICATION

I dedicate this book to children everywhere who want to learn about the world.
If you open your hearts and minds to new cultures and ideas, it will set you free.

When Christopher was two years old, a new baby sister, named Caroline, was born into his family. Caroline was a beautiful baby with red hair and green eyes. When she was only one month old, and Christopher was just three, their family moved to India.

India is a country like nowhere else in the world. It is a land with an ancient history, full of brilliant colors, rich sounds, amazing scenery, many religions, and more people than Christopher and Caroline had ever seen in their lives.

They moved into a big white home with a large garden dripping with colorful orange and purple bougainvillea flowers. Christopher especially loved the green parrots in the trees, and loved to put them on his shoulders.

Many people were hired to work at their house. There was Leela Aunty, the roly poly cook, who made delicious Indian meals of curries and lentils.

DAL MAKHANI

SAMOSA

IDLI

UPMA

PARATHA

MASALA DOSA

She also made them wonderful treats like " idlies", and breads like "puri" and "chapati," which the children loved to eat with their hands like the people in India do.

Their babysitter was a young beautiful girl named Jaya Aunty. She played with the children every day in the garden where they hunted for flowers and drew colorful designs of chalk, called "Kolams", placed at the entrance to their home to greet visitors.

They had a magic gardener named Sampat, who delighted Christopher and Caroline by bringing animals for them to play with--love birds, little baby chicks, a big cow,

and even a temple elephant who came often to their garden to bless the children by bopping them on the head with his big trunk. Indian people think that elephants are very special animals.

Often in the afternoons, Christopher and Caroline would play at the old colonial Madras Club, where their parents would play tennis and drink lime sodas on the sun-washed terrace.

Sometimes they would go with their Mommy out in a yellow three wheeled cart, called an auto-rickshaw.

As they drove around the town they could *see* women wearing colorful flowing dresses, called *saris*, of bright colors like pink, blue, or green.

Sometimes Jaya Aunty would even dress little Caroline up in a tiny sari, and put bangles on her arm and a red dot, called a bindi in the middle of her forehead.

Indian women wear beautiful saris and bindis in the middle of their foreheads.

15

They might also see a cow walking right in the middle of the road, where everyone let it stay because Indian people think cows are holy animals that mustn't be hurt, because they give milk to the people.

On each street corner they could see colorful Hindu temples filled with statues of many Hindu gods.

There is a god people pray to for education, a god for health, and Shiva, the Lord of the Dance.

They even have a big fat elephant god, called Ganesha, who people pray to for good luck.

20

People in India always take off their shoes when they go into a temple to pray, or when they enter their house.

THE SUN WORSHIP

In India, many people meditate to be peaceful and calm, or do yoga, a kind of exercise that helps people become strong and balanced.

COBRA POSE ☐

TREE POSE ☐

WARRIOR POSE ☐

PLOUGH POSE ☐

CHILD POSE ☐

Which of these fun yoga positions can you do?

There are both Hindu and Muslim holidays in India. There is the Hindu holiday called Pongal, which is a day to clean out the house and buy new clothes, and the Muslim holiday Ramadan, when people don't eat or drink all day, and pray to thank God for their blessings.

Another Hindu holiday is called Diwali -- a festival of light, when people decorate their homes with tiny candles, or small clay lamps.

But, you better watch out on Holi, another holiday when everyone throws off the dark days of winter and

Celebrates spring by throwing colors on each other.

India has a long history, but one of the most famous Indians is Mahatma Gandhi, who helped India become a free country.

He showed everyone that you can change the world by peaceful actions rather than by fighting.

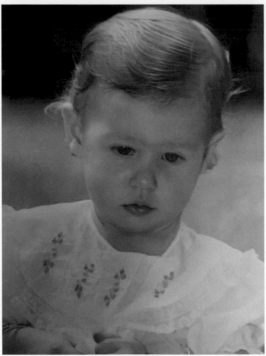

Christopher and Caroline loved living in India. It was a land of enchantment for them, so when they had to leave they were very sad.

But many years later, when they were both grown up, they were happy to go back there to see their old friends and work in the country that they loved so much.

Hopefully one day you, too, will go to India and discover this beautiful land for yourself!

The End

Printed in the United States
by Baker & Taylor Publisher Services